This book is dedicated to all the young
activists fighting for environmental justice
and a healthy future for Planet Earth. —L.R.

Many thanks to Lee Wade, Rachael Cole, Christopher Myers, Barbara Marcus,
Nicole de las Heras, Elyse Cheney, Derrick Alderman, Rick & Robin Redniss,
and Sasha, Theo, and Jody Rosen.

All rights reserved. Published in the United States by Random House Studio, an imprint of Random
House Children's Books, a division of Penguin Random House LLC, New York.

Random House Studio with colophon is a registered trademark of Penguin Random House LLC.

Visit us on the Web! rhcbooks.com

Educators and librarians, for a variety of teaching tools, visit us at RHTeachersLibrarians.com

Library of Congress Cataloging-in-Publication Data is available upon request.
ISBN 978-0-593-64594-9 (trade)
ISBN 978-0-593-64595-6 (lib. bdg.)
ISBN 978-0-593-64596-3 (ebook)

The artist used mixed media to create the images for this book.
The text of this book is set in 36-point Eusapia Paladino.

MANUFACTURED IN CHINA
10 9 8 7 6 5 4 3 2 1
First Edition

HEATWAVE

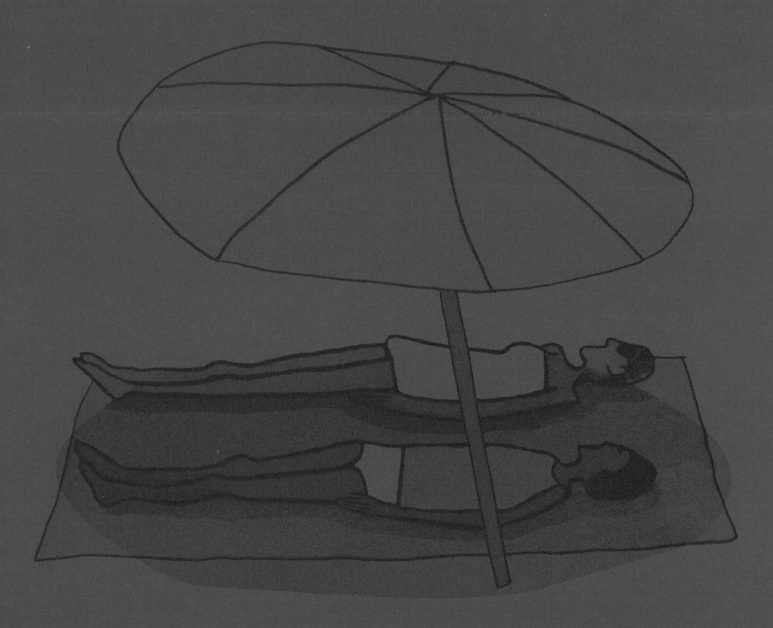

LAUREN REDNISS

RANDOM HOUSE STUDIO · NEW YORK

No way.

Too hot.

Game cancelled.

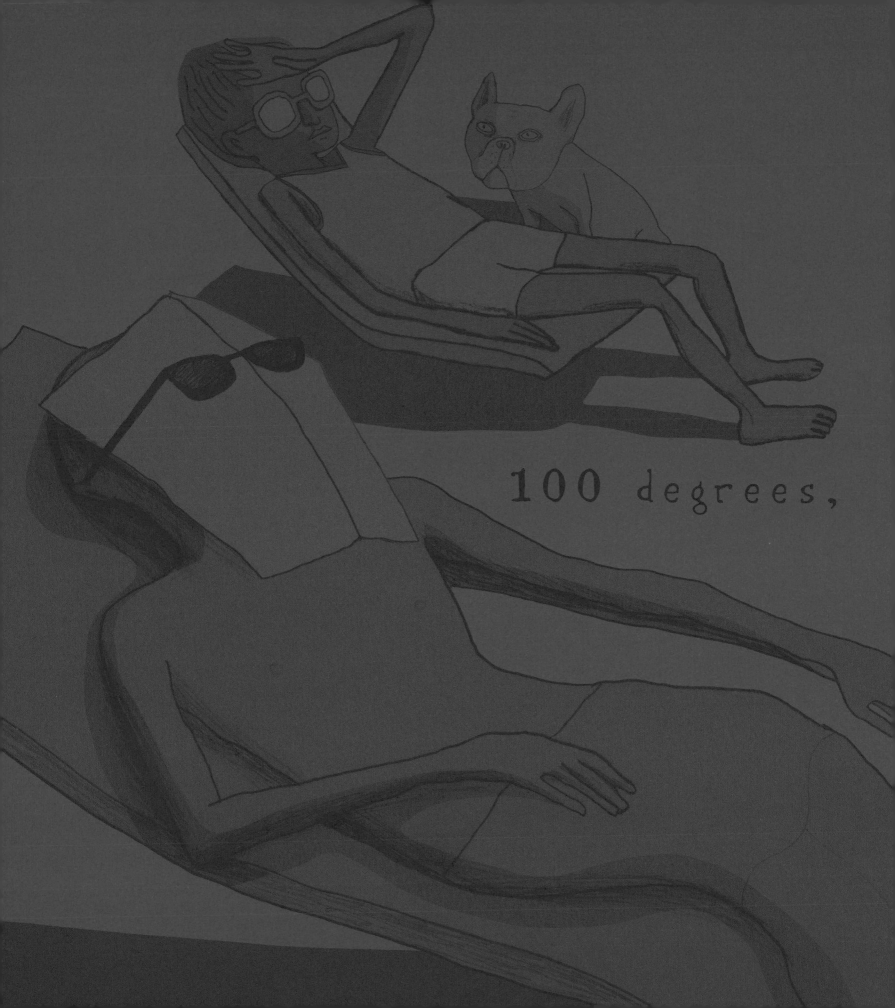

100 degrees,

in the shade.

Try not to burn.

Wind picks up.

Clouds roll in.

One raindrop.

Two.

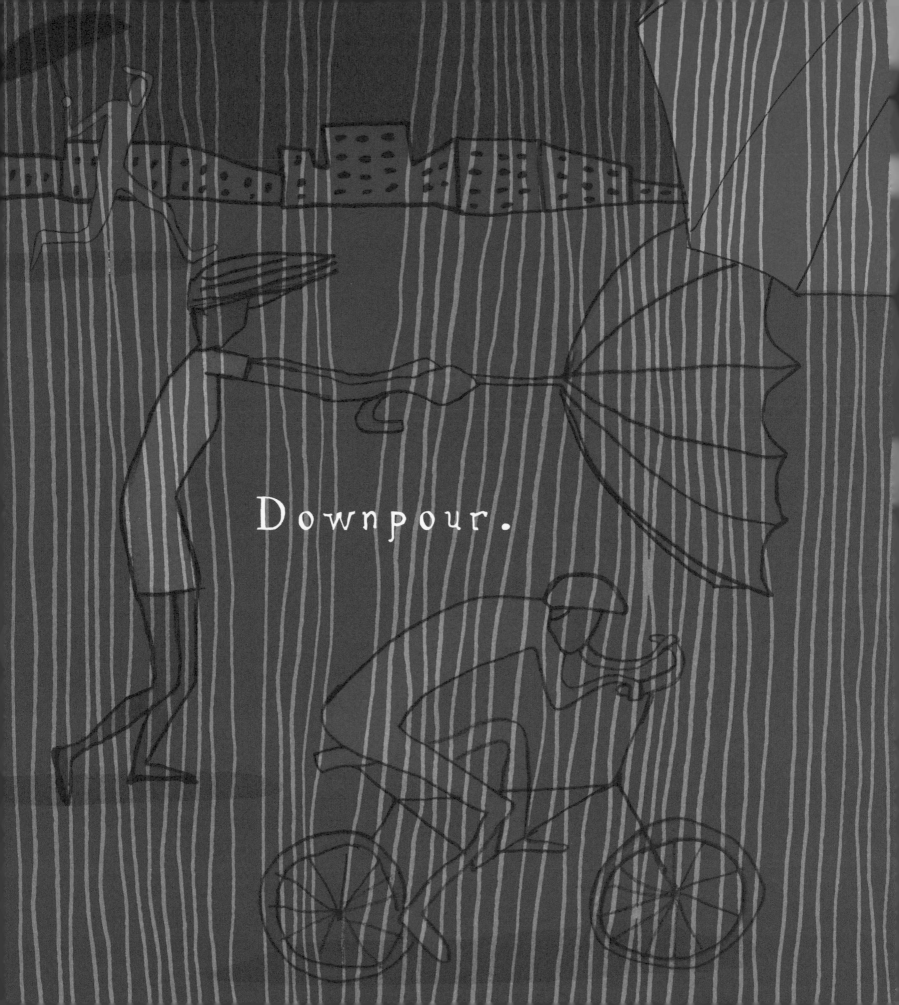

Downpour.

Run for cover.

Sun sets.

Moon rises.

Home.

Good night.